the coma

the coma

ALEX GARLAND

illustrations by Nicholas Garland

Riverhead Books · a member of Penguin Group (USA) Inc. · New York · 2004

RIVERHEAD BOOKS
a member of
Penguin Group (USA) Inc.
375 Hudson Street
New York, NY 10014

Library of Congress Cataloging-in-Publication Data

Garland, Alex, date.
The coma / Alex Garland ; illustrations by Nicholas Garland.
p. cm.
ISBN 1-57322-273-9
1. Coma—Patients—Fiction.   I. Title.
PR6057.A639C66   2004   2003069323
823'.914—dc22

Printed in the United States of America
1   3   5   7   9   10   8   6   4   2

This book is printed on acid-free paper. ♾

Book design by Claire Vaccaro

the coma

part one

U*ntil the telephone rang, the only sound in my office was the scratching of my pen as I made margin notes, corrections, and amendments.*

I pressed the speaker button.

"Carl speaking."

"Carl."

"Catherine! I meant to send you home hours ago—"

She interrupted me. "I am at home. I've been home, been out to see a film, eaten a pizza, paid the baby-sitter, and watched the end of Newsnight.*"*

The clock on my desk read 11:42. I turned in my chair. The window of my office was floor to ceiling. Through the window, I could see the city glitter and the night sky. No stars—a low cloud layer made the sky glow almost red.

Catherine continued. "I'm calling because the last tube leaves in twenty-five minutes."

. . .

At the underground station, I kept reading through papers. I made more notes in the margins, and the pen slipped as the papers buckled under the pressure of the nib. From somewhere, an echo of laughter bounced down the tiled walls and corridors. I looked up as the sound faded, but I was the only person on the platform. Even so, the noise unnerved me a little. It was humorless and predatory.

I folded my papers away—the loose pages in my hand made me feel vulnerable. As I closed my bag, closed the worn brass clasp, I felt a suck of air as my train approached.

The only other passenger on my carriage was a girl in her early twenties, sitting at the far end of the car, reading a book.

Just before the doors closed, I heard the laughter again. The noise was closer and clearer than the first time, but the platform was still empty—from what I could see of it, looking each way over my shoulder, tilting my head backwards towards the glass in order to increase my angle of sight. Then the doors closed and the train gave a slight lurch. I looked back at the girl. She was still immersed in her novel.

I stared ahead at my reflection in the opposite window and watched my head rock with the movement of the carriage.

·   ·   ·

When the train had reached its fastest speed, something appeared in my peripheral vision. A shadow in an area of lightness. I glanced in its direction, and saw that the faces of four young men had appeared through the dirt and thick glass of the doors between the carriages. Their heads were crowded into the frame of the window.

Moments later, the doors opened. As the men moved from their carriage to mine, everything was startling and loud. The pounding sound of the wheels on the tracks, the gasping sound of the subway walls as they rushed past.

The young men crowded the girl in the same way they had crowded the window. They leaned over her, hanging on the straps, blocking her from my view.

One of them reached down to grab the bag between her legs. There was a scuffle of some sort, which temporarily the girl seemed to win. She took her bag by the handle and stood, pushing the men aside. Most of this I saw from the corner of my eye.

The girl walked the full length of the carriage towards me and sat down, precisely blocking my reflection in the opposite window. She struck me as brave. I think it was that she was *still holding her book in one hand, and one finger was still keeping the page she had been reading.*

"Excuse me," she said. "Do you mind if I sit here?"

I shook my head and held her gaze and hoped my expression seemed reassuring. I didn't need to look sideways to know the young men would follow her down the carriage. I wondered what would happen next.

The young men appeared; one of them pulled at the girl's bag again; her wrist was grabbed; her arm was twisted in order to make her release her grip on the handle; she shouted.

I didn't feel sure of what was happening. I didn't know what to do.

I stood. I raised a hand. I said, "Hey."

As a small boy, I once fell backwards from a high swing and hit the back of my head hard on the ground. As this accident was happening, I watched it remotely, from the perspective of the branches of the tree to which the swing was tied.

Now, through the side windows of the train, as if I were hovering between the external glass and the subway walls, I saw myself walking backwards through the carriage, holding up my arms around my face and upper body. The young men were attacking me. Many of their blows looked as if they glanced harmlessly off my head and shoulders, and some missed me altogether. But some blows connected hard.

My movements seemed slow and confused. My hands swung out a couple of times to ward the men off, but the gesture looked no more fierce than if I was swatting away a fly. Soon my legs buckled, and I fell backwards against the seats, then rolled down to the floor. From my position outside the carriage, I watched as the young men kicked me into unconsciousness.

1.

Still as a remote viewer, I remained near my unconscious body. Not in continuous observation—I
saw myself in a series of slow snapshots that must have
been separated by several hours if not days.

In the first image, and the briefest, I saw myself in
the back of an ambulance. My shirt was open and cov-
ered in blood, and an oxygen mask was being held to
my face.

In the next image, I was lying on a hospital bed, in
what I imagine was an intensive care unit. I was still
wearing an oxygen mask; my head and chest were bandaged; I was connected to machines. Catherine, my
secretary, was sitting beside the bed, and she was cry-
ing. A male doctor stood behind her. He was reaching
towards her, as if about to make a gesture of comfort,
but he never seemed to cover the remaining few inches

to complete the gesture, and his fingers remained float-ing above her shoulder like a faith healer's.

In another image, I had been moved from the open ward to a private room, and the girl from the train carriage was in the room with me. She was holding a bunch of chrysanthemums and a card, and she looked uncomfortable. She spent more time looking at the flowers she held than at my face, which was now out of bandages, and showing its bruises, but sleeping peace-fully. The girl stayed with me a short while. Her lips moved occasionally, but I missed the words. Eventually she put the flowers in a vase and the card on my bedside table and left.

In the final image, a man—a nurse, I think—sat on my bed and talked to me, and as he talked he looked with great concentration at my face. Again, I couldn't hear the words, but from his posture and expressions I knew he was speaking in a very direct manner. I assume he was trying to wake me up.

The male nurse was still with me when I finally did wake up. Back in my body now, I opened my eyes with some effort, arching my eyebrows to pull the lids apart and break the sleep crust. A damp cloth or a sponge was wiped against my face. I asked for water, and the nurse put the lip of a glass to my mouth. When I swallowed, I felt as if I could trace precisely the path of the water down my throat. I thought I could feel it pooling in my stomach, and the surface rippling as I shifted my position.

"I am alive, then," I said eventually.

"Yes," said the male nurse.

"Am I badly injured?"

"You're recovering."

"Good," I said. "That's good to hear."

2.

Sometime later, I sat in a wheelchair and talked to two policemen. The older of the two did most of the speaking. He wanted to know if prior to the attack I had laid a hand on the young men, or assaulted them in any way.

"Absolutely not," I replied. "I mean, I was trying to stop them from robbing the girl. But all I did was stand up. The next thing I knew, they were punching me. I wouldn't have had time to assault them, even if I had wanted to."

The older policeman nodded. "That's no different from the statement of the witness."

"Was she hurt? The girl?"

"No."

"I was afraid she might have been raped."

"She wasn't hurt. They took her bag, but we recovered it when we arrested them."

"You caught them?"

I must have sounded surprised, because the younger policeman seemed to take offense.

"We do catch people sometimes," he said, with a little heat in his voice.

The older policeman continued. "When they jumped off at the next station, they'd been captured five different times on CCTV before they even reached street level. In fact, two of them we were able to track on camera right to the doors of their homes. They won't be getting away with this; you can rest assured of that."

"What about my bag?" I asked. "I had a bag. Did you recover that too?"

The older policeman frowned. "A bag?"

"Yes. With a brass clasp. It had papers inside."

The younger policeman started checking through his notepad. "I don't have any record of a bag with a brass clasp," he said. "It wasn't with you in the carriage."

"And I don't remember seeing any of them carrying a second bag on the CCTV," the older policeman added. "But we will look into it."

"It's very important I find the bag," I said. "I need it for my work."

"You shouldn't be worrying about your work for the moment," the older policeman said.

"You will try to find it, though? It had my wallet inside and it was full of papers and . . ."

"If I may," said the older policeman. "I think you should put all thought of work and papers out of your head. Your most important job right now is to get yourself better." He smiled at me. "Out of this hospital and back home."

3.

I was discharged the next evening. The hospital provided a taxi for me, and something to wear. My clothes had been torn and badly bloodstained in the attack, so as I walked up the steps to my house, I was wearing green pajamas and slippers.

I realized at once how long I must have lain unconscious in the hospital from the large pile of letters that the front door pushed aside. I carried the letters through to the living room and pressed "play" on my answering machine. I had thirty-four messages, but I didn't feel ready to listen to them, and I didn't feel ready to open my post either. I didn't even feel ready to turn on the lights. Instead, I turned on the television.

I watched the ten o'clock news. I had missed the headlines and the lead stories. I heard an account of a fire in a nightclub and saw an argument between two celebrities. The argument was outside a film premiere, and it had been caught by a member of the public on a videocamera. The newsreader speculated that although the celebrities had nearly come to blows, it was possible the argument had been staged as a promotional exercise. I thought, as I watched the newsreader, that he seemed quite uninterested in the truth behind the confrontation, because several times he seemed to lose the meaning of the words he was reading from the autocue—failing to anticipate the end of one sentence, or the beginning of another. I also suspected that he didn't recognize the celebrities any more than I did.

Like the newsreader, I lost concentration. When I regained it, the television program had changed to a black-and-white film. I turned the television off and went upstairs to bed.

I was reminded again of how long I had lain unconscious in the hospital by the dust in my bedroom. The bed was unmade—just as I had left it when I had gone to work the morning of the attack. When I tugged at the duvet, the dust stung my eyes like pollen and made me blink convulsively. I could feel the irritation in my nose and at the back of my throat.

But it was a warm night, so I pulled the duvet to the floor and opened the window to get a little fresh air circulating in the room. Then I stripped off the hospital pajamas, changed into some boxer shorts, and lay down.

I hadn't closed the curtains, so the room was bright from the street lamps outside. I wasn't really trying to get to sleep. During the cab ride from the hospital, I had felt apprehensive about what psychological fallout I might expect from the attack. It seemed to me that it would be at home that the fallout would make itself felt, as I tried to reintroduce myself to normality after such an abnormal and shocking incident. The familiarity of home would force a juxtaposition that the unfamiliar hospital had not. Specifically, I think I was concerned about nightmares—reliving the attack in a dream world, where perhaps the dream would loop endlessly, where the attack might be even more brutal and unpleasant than its real counterpart.

I had decided during the cab ride that the most sensible approach to the psychological fallout would be, in a sense, to keep my expectations low. I wouldn't have any plans or give myself any targets, such as returning to work within a set time. Where sleep was concerned, I wouldn't try for it, nor would I resist it if it came.

The cab driver, whom I'd spoken to a little during the journey from the hospital, had agreed.

"I was in a car crash once," he explained. "What they say is, after a car crash, you've got to get driving again or you'll lose your nerve. The same as if you fall off a horse. Or a bike. Or a ladder."

I nodded at the reflection of his eyes in his rearview mirror.

"But I did it differently," he continued. "After my car crash, when I got back in my cab for the first time, I didn't even turn on the engine."

We had pulled up at a traffic light at this point, so he turned around in his seat to emphasize the point.

"I didn't even touch the wheel!" He shook his head as the lights changed and we moved on. "My wife thought I was mad. She was watching me from the pavement. But I wasn't mad." He shook his head again. "And I didn't switch on the engine the second time either, but I did take off the hand brake. We live on a slight slope, so the cab moved forwards a couple of feet or so. Not more, because there was a parked car in front. 'You're mad!' my wife said. But look at me now. I'm driving again."

He was quiet for a few moments, then added, "It's okay to take things slowly."

4.

Although the room was reasonably bright from the street lamps, I didn't become aware that blood was seeping through my bandages until I rolled onto my side and felt the under sheet sticking to my back. I had felt the wetness already, but assumed it was sweat from the warm night. I sat up in bed and saw a large dark stain on the linen, and when I put my hand to the bandages, they were sodden. Alarmed, I went straight to my bathroom and switched on the light.

In the mirror, I was swaddled in red. I must have opened several cuts without realizing—cuts I hadn't even known I'd had. I had no real idea of the injuries to my chest; the bandages around my torso had not been changed since I had woken up. Until seeing the blood, I'd assumed the bandages were to cover the bruises that spread up around the top of the wrapping, over my collarbone and up to my face.

But now, inspecting myself more carefully in the mirror, I could see that the bruises I had seen in the hospital had faded to the point where I wasn't sure if I was seeing discoloration on the skin surface or simply shadows thrown by the overhead halogen bulbs. Certainly, as I moved my head and re-angled my body, the marks that looked like bruises seemed to change, and if I angled my body backwards, to lean up towards the light, my skin seemed entirely clear.

Meanwhile, the blood was seeping down from the bandages into the elasticized waistband at the top of my boxer shorts. I decided I should remove the wrapping as quickly as possible and assess the seriousness of the wounds. If they looked bad, the only sensible thing would be to return to the hospital.

They did look bad. That is to say—they appeared bad. I was as good as painted red, a great block of color from the top of my chest to my navel. But as I peeled off the last strip of soaked material and let it drop to my feet, I could see that the appearance was thankfully deceiving. I couldn't actually see a wound—from a stab or a

slice or a graze—anywhere. In a way, this didn't surprise me. I had often heard that the blood from wounds
could be misleading as to their seriousness. And I felt
fine; not dizzy, or in pain, or even in discomfort.

I stood over the sink and wiped away the blood
with a towel. My only remaining concern was to find
the source of the bleeding and to dress it properly—
and I guessed that a well-applied Band-Aid would do
the job. It had probably been the looseness of the bandages that had encouraged the bleeding.

An idea struck me. Like falling from the swing, it
was another memory from childhood—this time, of re-
pairing punctures on my bike. A cut in the rubber was
also impossible to spot with the eye. The only options
were to turn the inner tube slowly against your ear and
listen for the sound of hissing, or to place the entire inner tube in water, where you would see the escaping air
as a stream of bubbles.

I didn't think I would be hissing, and even a black
belt in yoga wouldn't be able to get an ear to his own
chest, so I ran a bath.

From a point on my solar plexus, a miniature tendril of
blood seeped into the water, like a faint coral or a sea

anemone. The wound must have been no larger than a pinprick.

As my gaze flicked between the coral, and the congealing puddle of bandages on the bathroom floor, and the red smears around the basin and the chrome taps, I began to think for the first time that my psychological fallout might be more severe than I had anticipated.

5.

I leaned on Anthony's doorbell. It was well past midnight and all the lights in his house were off, as were the lights in the houses of his neighbors, and as far down the street as I could see. When he came to the door he was wearing a dressing gown and all the hair on the left-hand side of his head was sticking directly up into the air.

"Carl," he said. Then again. "Carl! God. What time is it? Are you okay?"

"I think so," I replied. "More or less. But I need to come in."

"Of course, of course," he said, collecting himself, smoothing down his hair and rubbing the sleep and surprise out of his eyes.

I followed him inside to the kitchen.

. . .

"I'm sorry for waking you," I said, as Anthony filled the kettle with water from the tap. "Did I wake Mary as well? And Joshua?"

Anthony shrugged. "Mary will be back to sleep already. Joshua—I don't know. It doesn't matter. Anyway, I'm the one who's sorry. I meant to collect you from the hospital today. I knew you were being discharged, but . . ." He turned to me. "Well—but nothing. I should have been there."

"I don't think I wanted to be collected. I wanted to go home alone, to keep everything low key. Now I'm not so sure. Maybe it wasn't such a good idea."

Anthony leaned back against the counter and waited for me to continue. But I didn't continue. I wasn't quite sure what I ought to say. So we both waited, while steam from the kettle began to rise and collect under the kitchen units.

Eventually I said, "If we wait long enough, something strange will happen."

Anthony frowned. "What do you mean?"

"Just . . . that. If we wait long enough, something strange will happen. I suspect I'll be the only one who notices it. So perhaps it will only be strange to me . . ."

"Strange?"

"Strange."

"Tell me what you mean."

"Well, for example, I don't know how I got here tonight."

". . . To my house?"

"To your house—yes. I have no idea. I don't even remember making a decision to come here. One moment I was lying in the bath, the next I was ringing your doorbell. With nothing in between, except . . ." I shook my head in a gesture of helplessness. "A transition of some sort."

"A blackout?"

"Probably. It's the most likely explanation. But . . ." I paused a moment. "How *did* I get here tonight? Did I drive? Is my car parked outside?"

Anthony glanced out the kitchen window. "No. It isn't."

"So did I walk? It would have taken me forty minutes at least. The buses and the tubes aren't running." I felt in my pockets. "And I don't have my wallet. I couldn't have paid for a cab."

We fell into a short silence again, with Anthony watching me in a slightly puzzled or troubled way. Then the kettle clicked off.

"We don't have milk, so the coffee will have to be black," Anthony said. "Sorry about that."

I shook my head to show my lack of concern. Or lack of interest.

"No," Anthony said, quite firmly, as if correcting my noncommittal response. "It's a pity. Fresh milk, fresh coffee. Some things are just meant for each other."

"Okay."

He poured two mugs and put sugar on the table, then sat opposite me.

"So. If we wait, how long do you think it will take before something strange happens?"

"Your guess is certainly as good as mine," I said.

Anthony smiled. "Okay, then. We'll just wait."

6.

I didn't want to drink the coffee. It looked dark and
bitter, and there was a thin rainbow film on the surface. I think it was the residue of detergent. It made the
liquid slightly iridescent, like the back of a beetle or an
oil slick.

And milk wouldn't have helped. Milk or irides-
cence aside, I didn't want to drink the coffee because I
didn't much care for the taste—and never had. In fact,
I felt mildly irritated that Anthony had given me the
mug in the first place, because, considering our friend-
ship, I thought my dislike of coffee was the sort of
thing he ought to know.

The more I thought about it, the more peculiar the
coffee became. Then, as I stared into the unwanted
mug, it struck me abruptly that perhaps this—the unwanted mug—was the strange thing I had predicted

would happen. The strange thing already *had* happened. It was happening even as I was making the prediction.

The idea was interesting, and also frustrating—I had hoped that the strange thing would be more spectacular. As spectacular as blood-soaked bandages and bed sheets. In comparison, as an illustration of an unusual event, the making and offering of coffee seemed to err on the side of subtlety. Worse, in attempting to convey its strangeness to Anthony, I might come across as altogether too intense—too deep into the analysis of a hot drink. The only thing that would seem strange was me.

On cue, Anthony said, "Don't you want your coffee?"

I looked up from the mug to face him.

7.

"Oh!" I said.

Behind Anthony, the fronts of the houses opposite were dark, in shadow from a sun that was still too low to be seen above the rooftops. But the sky was a clear blue, and light was flooding into the kitchen. Birds were singing.

"There." I leaned forwards across the table. "There! That's what I'm talking about!"

Anthony stared back at me. "What are you talking about?"

"What am I—?" I broke off, pushing back my chair, and went to the window. "It's *dawn*! There's light flooding into the room. There's a milk float down the road."

"I know it's dawn," Anthony said.

"So that's it! That's the strange thing! A moment ago it was dark, it was the middle of the night, and I was looking at the coffee, and now—"

"Just a minute," Anthony interrupted. "Did you say that the milk float is outside?"

"Yes!"

"Sorry, Carl," said Anthony, rising hurriedly, and he almost ran out of the room. "I must catch the milk-man before he goes," he called from the hall.

A few moments later, I watched through the window as Anthony jogged across his front lawn in his dressing gown, holding a twenty-pound note in the air like an Olympic torch.

I felt a sudden and terrific feeling of despair.

I knew that feeling. When I was a little boy, around five or six, I would have very powerful fever dreams. They always seemed to involve scale—in a beige landscape, I would feel overwhelmed by a sense of the amazingly huge or the unbearably small. So, in the landscape, I would be small while the landscape was limitless and enormous. Or I would be huge while the landscape was claustrophobic and confining. Or both conditions would exist simultaneously, which was clearly impossible yet apparently the case.

The beige landscape might be a flat plain. As a vast form, I might be a gigantic ball or sphere, far bigger than a planet or a sun. In my hands, or through my fingers, I would feel the hard corners and edges of cubes and pyramids, or the smooth curved surface of another gigantic sphere. Everything was represented in terms of geometry. Everything was flux. All of these states and sensations were extremely disturbing.

Looking back on these dreams, I can rationalize that they were related to my parents' bed, where I would be put to sleep if running a high temperature. I would be semi-asleep, perhaps semi-delirious, and the hugeness would be the distance from one side of the mattress to the other. The confinement would be the heavy duvet weighing down on my body. The hard corners and smooth surfaces would be the wooden bedframe or the sheets.

It's less easy to rationalize why I found the dreams so disturbing. I know I was running a high temperature, which is disturbing in itself, if only for being so physically uncomfortable. But there was something more than that—something that, to the mind of a five- or six-year-old, was particularly frightening. While I was locked into the dream, I had a very strong sense that the landscape was real. Moreover, that the landscape of geometry and flux and impossible scale was the *only* real landscape. That all other landscapes, including the one that held my parents and brother, were an illusion superimposed on the beige plains, and false.

"Carl?"

I turned. Mary was standing in the doorway, holding their son, Joshua, in her arms.

"Hi, Mary," I said.

"Where's Anthony?"

"Outside." I gestured towards the window. "He's paying the milkman."

"Good. I've been getting on at him to do that for ages." Mary smiled and walked into the kitchen. "So," she said, scanning the food inside the fridge, half balancing Joshua on her hip. "Are you going to be staying for breakfast?"

"I hadn't thought as far as breakfast," I replied. "This morning has sort of taken me by surprise."

8.

Mary's back was to me. She was standing by the sink, beating two eggs in a bowl. Beside her, on the cooker, a whole pack of bacon and some fat mushrooms were frying in a pan. A second, smaller pan was melting butter over the flame.

I held a glass of orange juice in my hand. Joshua had orange juice too, in a closed child's mug. He sat opposite in a high chair, watching me with wide dark eyes.

Outside, Anthony continued to talk to the milkman. I could see them both through the window, over Mary's shoulder, and they looked as if they were sharing a joke.

"Mary," I said, making an effort to keep an even tone to my voice. "Have you ever had a nervous breakdown?"

Mary stopped beating the eggs and poured them straight into the smaller pan. "Scrambled or fried," she said. "Quick decision required."

"Scrambled," I said, when I realized she wasn't talking about my state of mind.

Mary began pushing the eggs around with a wooden spoon. "Yes, I had a breakdown. Years ago, now. I was in my mid-twenties."

"Do you remember it well?"

"Hardly at all. I remember that it ended with a stay in the hospital."

"Mine seems to have begun with a stay in the hospital."

"Okay," said Mary. "This is why you arrived here in the middle of the night."

"Yes."

"You're afraid you might be having a breakdown."

"That's right."

"Is it to do with the attack?"

"I think so. I think I've been traumatized. Psychologically." I took a gulp of my orange juice, and Joshua mirrored the movement, raising and lowering his hand at the same moment. "Since I was discharged, I've been hallucinating pretty much constantly."

"Hallucinating?" said Mary, sounding surprised.

She pulled the eggs off the heat and turned to me. "Seeing things?"

"Yes."

"That sounds quite . . ." She looked for the word. "Extreme."

"It is," I agreed, and I saw her gaze flick to Joshua.

"I'm not a danger to anyone," I said quickly.

"Are you hallucinating now?"

I shrugged. "I don't know. Are you a hallucination?"

"Not as far as I know."

"Okay, so—if I take your word for it—then I'm not hallucinating now."

Mary nodded. Then she said, "Tell me about the things you've been seeing."

I told her about the blood and the bandages, and the blackouts, and the sudden dawn.

When I had finished, Mary thought for a few moments, then asked, "Are you depressed?"

I shook my head.

"Did the doctors put you on any kind of medication?"

"No."

Mary looked at me hard, straight into my eyes, as if she might be able to see past them through to the confusion in my head. "Well, Carl," she said. "I'm no expert, but you don't sound to me like you're having a nervous breakdown. And you don't come across like it either."

"That's good news."

Mary opened her mouth, but hesitated.

"Or is it?" I said.

"I don't know," she replied. Then she lowered her voice, as if a softer tone would be less likely to alarm me. "Have you wondered if perhaps your hallucinations aren't the result of psychological damage?"

"Go on," I said.

"As I said, Carl, I'm not an expert. But—you were knocked unconscious."

"I know I was," I said impatiently. "What are you getting at?"

Mary's voice softened further. "What if the damage is neurological?"

Joshua put a hand to the side of his head, echoing my movements again.

". . . What if you have brain damage?"

"Brain damage," I echoed. It seemed so obvious and so plausible that I don't how I had failed to consider it until now.

"I'm sorry," said Mary. "I don't mean to be so blunt, but . . ."

"No," I replied distantly. "Not at all."

"What are you going to do?"

"I don't know," I said. "I suppose I should have a scan . . ."

"I think that has to be sensible," said Mary. "At the very least, you need to talk to a doctor."

"Yes," I said. "I should leave at once. Return to the hospital."

"That would probably be best," Mary agreed.

9.

"Leaving?" asked Anthony when I passed him on the front lawn. He was still talking to the milkman.

"Yes," I said. "I'm going to the hospital."

I waited a moment, imagining that Anthony would offer me a lift. But instead he gave me the thumbs-up.

"Good idea," he said. "Listen, let me know how it works out."

"I will," I said irritably. "Thanks for all your help."

Either he didn't notice the sarcasm, or he decided to let it go.

The milkman's float was parked in the early morning sunshine, now that the sun had risen over the rooftops. The milk was warming. You could smell it in the air and see it in the droplets of condensation on the sides of the glass bottles.

Judging by the blue and cloudless sky, it was going to be a beautiful day.

10.

I'd been walking five minutes before I remembered that I couldn't catch the train or get a cab because I didn't have my wallet, and I had forgotten to borrow any money from Anthony or Mary. I considered walking back, but I was feeling increasingly upset at Anthony for his blasé reaction to my condition, and I thought that if I saw him again that morning we might end up having an argument. So I kept going. I didn't think it would take me longer than an hour to reach the hospital on foot, and I felt I could use the time to think.

I tried to think with clarity.

I was probably not suffering from psychological trauma, as I had at first suspected. Instead, as Mary had pointed out, it was more likely that I had some kind of brain damage. Which, to look on the bright side, might be reversible. Even, in some ways, easier to address than psychological trauma—or at least more straightforward. A blood clot between my skull and gray matter could be removed, relieving pressure and bringing a return of normal function. If so, the removal of the blood clot might be a matter of urgency, and by walking slowly to the hospital I was wasting the minutes that were required to save me from permanent brain damage, or even to save my life.

But I didn't pick up my pace. I suppose I was being fatalistic, and it simply seemed more likely to me that the damage was irreversible, in which case it made no difference how long I took to get to the hospital. And perhaps it was not only irreversible but stable. In which case I had to consider whether I could successfully operate in the world while in a state of rolling hallucination.

Would it be possible to hold down a job when continuously uncertain whether it was the middle of the night or mid-morning? Would it be possible to have a relationship with friends whose behavior was inexplicable to me? Looking to the future, would I ever be able

to achieve the most basic ambitions of finding a partner
and having a family?

Given my experiences over the last twelve hours,
which I wasn't even sure constituted twelve hours, the
answers to all these questions seemed to be no. I
couldn't imagine being a father if, on arriving at school
to collect my kids at the end of the day, I was unable to
establish whether I was at a school or at a petrol station. I might not even be able to feel sure of the iden-
tities of my children. I might have to wait at the front
gates, scanning the small faces, looking for ones that
were looking back at me with an expression of familiarity or expectancy.

The implications of my condition began to ex-
plode. It occurred to me suddenly that, for all I knew, I
already had a wife and family and I had hallucinated
myself into a state where they didn't exist. I cursed myself for having left my wallet at home. I could have
checked it for passport-sized photos or crayon drawings
of houses with smiling stick figures standing outside.

In fact, the implications were almost limitless. If I
couldn't differentiate between hallucination and reality, it was hard to conceive of anything certain I could
use to define myself. I might be a different age from the

age I believed I was, or a different gender. I might not be walking down a street but standing in a field, or lying in a room. At that moment, on my slow walk to the hospital, it seemed to me that everything was up for grabs. I could be anything with a consciousness.

A volley of car horns broke me out of the train of thought.

Anthony and Mary lived in a middle-class suburb of houses and lawns, and hedges, and windows with diamond-shaped lattices made of lead—and many of those who lived in these houses were starting their commute to work. It seems that one of these commuters was attempting to turn his car in the road. The flow of traffic was stopped in both directions.

I watched as the driver drove a few feet forwards, then backwards, then forwards again, each time managing to bring the car a few degrees around. The horns grew angrier and more varied as more cars joined in, and the three-point turn became a five, then six, then seven. The extra noise seemed to fluster the driver, who made several forwards and reverse moves that hardly rotated the car at all. But eventually the driver found the space to straighten up, and, over-revving first gear wildly, brought the car lurching back down the road in my direction.

Then, to my surprise, it drew alongside me and braked sharply—smoking its two front tires and provoking another volley of horns from the cars behind.

The front passenger door swung open, and the driver, whose face I couldn't see, called for me to get inside.

11.

"Would you put your seat belt on?" the driver said, and he accelerated hard.

As I reached for the seat belt, the driver spun the wheel to turn down a side street, throwing me against the passenger window.

"Sorry," the driver said. "We're in a hurry."

I pulled the seat belt across me as fast as I could before he took another corner at the same speed. Which he did, just as I managed to guide the buckle home.

"Do you remember me?" the driver asked. I looked sideways. The man's face was in profile; he was concentrating hard on the road ahead. In some ways the profile did look familiar, but I couldn't place it.

"No," I said. "But don't take offense. The way things are, you could be my brother for all I know."

"I'm not your brother."

The driver braked quite hard for another corner, and I raised a hand to brace against the dashboard. This time when he swung the car around, we were turning off the residential streets and on to a slip road, joining a dual carriageway.

"Or my aunt," I added. "You could be anyone."

"I'm not your aunt either," he said. "I gave you water. I helped you to sit up."

I looked at the driver again. And this time I made the connection. It was the expression of concentration on his face—the same expression I had seen when the man was sitting by my bed at the hospital, talking to me, trying to wake me up.

"I do remember you," I said. "You're the nurse."

"Yes," he confirmed. "I'm the nurse."

I glanced over at the dashboard. The needle on the speedometer was climbing fast. It passed sixty, then seventy, then eighty, then ninety.

"We really are in a hurry," I said. "Where are we going?"

"Hospital," the nurse replied, using the inside lane to overtake a string of cars.

"Then I am in trouble. My condition is going to deteriorate."

"It may."

I nodded. So much for relaxed fatalism, I thought, and felt a little surge of panic—which was not helped by the way in which our car was continuing to gain speed, now creeping past one hundred. "What happened?" I asked, injecting calm into my voice. "I imagine Mary or Anthony called the hospital and explained to you about my condition, and you tracked down to—"

He cut me off. "Carl—there isn't time for me to answer your questions. I need to ask you questions."

"Of course," I said. "Diagnosis. Okay."

"Can you tell me what day it is?"

I thought for a moment. I wasn't entirely surprised that I couldn't provide the answer. In the best of health, I've lost track of the days. "No," I replied.

"Or what year it is?"

". . . No."

"What can you tell me about your work?"

I thought again. And this time, I did feel surprised by the blankness I felt in response to the question. "I work with papers," I said hesitantly. "I keep the papers in a briefcase with a brass clasp. And I work in a tall building. Somewhere in the center of . . . the city."

"What city?"

I looked out the window at the high-rise flats that lined the dual carriageway. "I don't know what city this is," I said. And this time the surge of panic was unstoppable.

I felt as if I had been standing on the walkway of a dam that was breaking. And now it was broken. The endlessly rising speed of the car was my ejection on a plume of water.

And for a while, something that I knew was pure hallucination gripped me entirely, as the cars on the road became tumbling blocks of concrete and the road became tumbling foam, and the engine noise became the roar of a torrent that enveloped me.

12.

"We're here," said the nurse.

I looked around. We had stopped. We were at the hospital.

"Is there time to save me?" I asked.

"I hope so," the nurse replied.

"Thank you," I said. My voice was shaking. "For helping me. For coming to find me."

The nurse smiled. "It's my job."

"What's your name? I'd like to know it."

The nurse paused. "You don't know my name," he said. "So I can't tell you what it is."

I didn't understand, and he didn't give me a chance to ask him to explain. He reached across me and opened the side door. "Come on," he said. "We should go."

part two

1.

I was led through the hospital by the nurse, down generic corridors and up disinfected stairwells. The nurse walked quickly and didn't talk.

In one ward, a radio was playing over the speaker system, but the volume had been turned down so low that the words of the DJ were inaudible. The patients here were all suffering from injuries to their hands. Every one of them was fully bandaged from the elbows down, and their arms were attached to wires that held them upwards.

In another ward, I saw that all the patients' beds were enclosed in plastic tents, as if quarantined. I could see their blurred forms through the sheeting. One figure was sitting up in bed. The man's head followed us as we passed.

Finally we came to a pair of swinging doors, and the nurse stopped. Above the doors a sign read: COMA WARD. The nurse looked back at me and gave a slight smile of encouragement. Then we walked in.

Off a single windowless corridor were twelve rooms, six down each side. The floor was carpeted. The lights in the corridor were dimmed.

"Do you have any memory of this place?" the nurse said quietly.

"I think so," I replied. "A little. It feels . . . familiar."

"Go on."

I breathed in through my nose. "It *smells* familiar. The flowers that people leave for the sick. And . . . dust, or . . ." I suddenly remembered the way my eyes had smarted when I lay down in my bed at home. "Pollen."

I took a few steps and glanced in the first door on my right. Inside, I noticed that the lighting was brighter. The patient, a woman, was lying on her side. No machines or wires were attached to her. There was no drama in the sight—she simply looked as if she were asleep.

When I looked through the open door on my left,

however, the patient was propped up on pillows, and clearly awake. The man, who I'd guess was in his twenties, had his eyes open, and his mouth open, and he appeared to be gazing around the room.

The nurse reacted to my expression with a little shake of his head.

"Comas like his can be very difficult for the family," he whispered.

"He isn't awake?"

"No."

Looking harder, I saw that the various directions of the man's gaze had no purpose. They were circular and repeating, and without focus.

"He's not seeing anything," I said.

"On a scan, there will be no real activity in his brain. It's the big difference between him and her." The nurse gestured back at the sleeping woman on the right. "And you," he added, and continued down the corridor.

At the far end, at the final door, which was closed, the nurse turned.

"This is your room," he said.

"I'll be staying here?" I asked.

"You are staying here," the nurse replied, and indicated for me to enter.

2.

This is the way it is with dreams. One moment I was opening the door to the ward room and seeing myself lying on the bed.

I was lying on the bed. The bruises I thought had faded and gone were covering my head and shoulders. My eyes were purple and yellow and puffed shut, and my lips were split. A support collar was fastened around my neck.

On the table, the flowers that had been left for me were starting to wilt. One of the heads had fallen and looked as if it had hit my pillow before rolling down to the floor. A spray of orange pollen showed where it had landed.

The next moment, I was lying on the bed. *I was lying on the bed, and the nurse was walking across the room towards me.*

He sat on the edge of the mattress.

"*Carl*," he said. "*Can you hear me?*"

"Yes," I said, and my mouth didn't move.

"*Carl, can you hear me?*"

His voice was loud and penetrating, but even in tone. The way you talk to the hard of hearing.

"Yes." My voice was equally loud and clear. "I can hear you."

Loud and clear, but completely internal.

The nurse lifted my hand and put it in his. His fingers felt strong. His clasp felt warm and dry.

"*If you can hear me, Carl, I'd like you to squeeze. Can you do that for me? Squeeze as hard as you can.*"

"Yes," I said.

"*Can you squeeze my hand for me, Carl?*"

"I am squeezing."

"Try as hard as you can."

"I am."

"Okay, Carl."

The nurse relaxed his grip, and my hand slipped out of his like a dead man's.

"Okay, Carl," he said again, but quieter this time. More to himself. *"We'll try again tomorrow."*

This is the way it is with dreams.

Not for the first time in this dream, I woke up.

3.

I woke up with my mouth open as if I was screaming, sitting upright in bed, soaked in sweat the same way I'd been soaked in blood.

Catherine, beside me, sat up too.

"Jesus," Catherine said. "Carl—what?" She had a tangle of hair hanging over her face, and she tripped over her words slightly. Sleep and adrenaline were clashing with each other. "What is it? What's wrong?"

"I'm dreaming."

"No, sweetheart, no. You *were* dreaming. You're awake now. It's okay. I'm right next to you."

"I'm awake?"

"Yes, yes."

Catherine put her hand in mine and squeezed. I squeezed back.

"I thought," I said. "I thought I was . . ."

I looked around me. I was in my bedroom. The window was open, and the curtains were pushed inwards by a breeze. A warm breeze, a warm night. On the bedside table, the clock read three in the morning, and the glow from the digital display lit the underside of a bunch of chrysanthemums, which stood in a vase.

"Was it a bad dream?" Catherine asked. She was properly awake now. We both were. "Tell me."

"A bad dream. Jesus—a terrible dream. I feel as if I've been dreaming for days. Maybe months. I've never had a dream like it."

"Tell me," she said again. "It will make it go away."

I shook my head. "I don't know how I'd begin."

She leaned forwards and kissed me. "Try."

"Okay," I said. "I—"

I broke off.

When Catherine had leaned forwards to kiss me, I had caught a slight scent of her perfume. And as I caught the scent, I also caught a half-memory, similar to the half-memories of falling from the garden swing or mending bicycle punctures. A window on a fragment of a moment, nothing revealed on either side of the window, no context. But inside the frame, something that felt strong and true.

This was the half-memory: sometimes when Catherine came into my office, the scent of her perfume would remain after she had left. The scent would distract me pleasantly and pull me away from work for a short while, leading me into a daydream.

I kissed Catherine back, and she responded, kissing me harder and lifting her hand to the side of my face. Then I pulled away.

"The daydream," I said, "was that the two of us were having an affair."

". . . Your terrible dream?"

"No. In my office, I would daydream that the two of us were having an affair."

"I don't understand. Why would you daydream about that?"

The curtains blew fully open for a brief moment, and the light from the street lamps outside illuminated half of Catherine's face. She was smiling at me.

"Exactly," I said carefully. "Why would I daydream about that?"

Catherine laughed. "You wanted the frisson. A simple relationship wasn't enough."

"No. I daydreamed because we didn't have a relationship."

The curtains had drifted shut again and her face was back in shadow, but I knew she was frowning. "I don't understand, Carl. I really don't understand what you're talking about. Look—you've just woken from a nightmare. You're confused, and you're confusing me—"

"Why are we in bed together?" I interrupted.

"Why?"

"Are we married?"

"No—we're not married. We're . . . together."

"Together."

"Yes."

"We share each other's lives."

She shrugged. "Yes."

"What's my job?"

She hesitated.

"What work do I do in my office? It's a simple question. Either as my secretary or my partner, you must know my job. What is it?"

She didn't answer.

I reached over and switched on the reading light to see her face and expression more clearly. And her face was blank as I repeated the question, and she still didn't answer.

4.

"It's taken me some time," I said. "I don't know how much time. But I think I've just managed to understand what's going on."

We were in the bathroom now. Catherine was wearing one of my T-shirts and sitting, knees together, arms folded as if she was cold, on the toilet seat. I was sitting on the edge of the bath. We faced each other over the pile of bandages I had left on the tiled floor.

"I never woke up."

I took a moment to further order my thoughts while Catherine waited patiently.

"I was attacked on a tube train on the way home from work, and I was put into a coma. And I never woke up. I just dreamed that I had."

"This is your terrible dream."

"It's all my terrible dream. Waking, being interviewed by the police, going back home, going to Anthony's . . . and lying in bed next to you. Sitting in a bathroom opposite you. But in truth . . ." I tried to be more precise. ". . . Or in reality, none of these things have happened. In reality, I'm lying in a hospital bed, with flowers on the side table, and falling pollen, and this is the dream I'm having while I sleep."

Catherine nodded.

"Right," I said. "You're nodding, because I'm not telling you anything you don't understand as well as I do. You know why?" I didn't wait for a reply. "Because you're not Catherine. I'm not talking to Catherine. I'm dreaming of Catherine. In effect, I'm talking to my-self." I started to smile at this train of thought, more from the relief of jigsaw pieces finding places than from pleasure. "You don't know what my job is because I don't know what my job is."

Catherine cocked her head to the side. "Why don't you know what your job is, Carl?" she asked.

"I don't know. From the blow to the head that put me in a coma, maybe. It's given me amnesia, or . . ."

Catherine's cocked head, the thoughtful expression on her face as she listened, her slim legs curling out from under the T-shirt, distracted me. I was reminded of how pretty she was.

"I wonder," I said. "At this moment, the real Catherine may be talking to the person who has replaced me at the office. Briefing them on the job that neither of us can remember. And if that person is anything like me, he's already starting to daydream about you. Started trying to place your scent."

Catherine dipped her eyebrows as if she found the idea distasteful. "I don't know why you say that," she said. "At this moment, the real Catherine might be sitting beside your bed in the hospital. She might care about you as much as you care for her. It may have been her that brought you the flowers."

"That's a nice thought." I looked at her a moment. "You're the best thing that's happened in this dream so far."

"Thank you," she said simply.

"Ah," I said. "I just remembered something else. You've always been good at accepting a compliment."

We fell into silence for a few moments, and when the silence lifted, we were back in the bedroom. Catherine had pulled open the curtains, and it was morning again.

"So what are you going to do, Carl?" she asked.

I shrugged. "What everyone in a coma has to do," I said. "I have to wake up."

5·

I had an idea: a layman's guide to waking from a coma. The idea took the form of an image—coma patients sprawled on hospital beds while people sat beside them, reading from books or playing passages of music on portable tape machines. Family members and friends, trying to infiltrate a catalyst into the coma patient's mind. Triggers, cascades, to lift the sleeper out of unconsciousness.

I mentioned this to Catherine just before the dream began to relocate me. As I was leaving her, and the bedroom, and the open curtains, I said: "I need a catalyst."

"What kind of catalyst?" Catherine asked.

"I don't know. I could listen to some records, maybe."

She said, "So go to a record shop," which was clearly excellent advice.

. . .

The understanding that I was sleeping made much greater sense of these relocations. Whereas previously I had mistaken them for blackouts, and felt unsure retrospectively how I might have moved from a bathtub to Anthony's front door, I now recognized them as familiar aspects of a dream life: that one moment you are here, and another you are there.

Very familiar. I could estimate I had spent perhaps a third of my life asleep, and a large proportion of that time must have been spent dreaming.

So: I *knew* dream life. In fact, in a way, I was actually comfortable with it. Dream life, I realized, was only confusing when you were awake. It was from the perspective of waking life that dream life seemed fractured and lacking consequence, lacking any certainty that one thing led to another. But from within dream life, the world was generally coherent. Not exactly an unconfusing world—just no more confusing than any other.

And now that I *knew* I was dreaming, had become self-aware, I had time to notice the details of how the relocations occurred. Catherine did not vanish like a ghost startled by daylight. Instead, the sense that I was sharing a space with her began to fade. And as that sense faded, so did the image.

Likewise, the bedroom. The place I was seeing was a sense of place. While I could sense it, I could see it. And if, as I shifted from one location to another, I could sense two places . . .

If I could sense a bedroom and open curtains, but also sense a record shop, with strip neon lighting and shelves of stacked LPs, alphabetized . . .

Then for a moment, curtains would blow open over the window of the record shop, and the vase of flowers would stand on the record shop counter.

6.

There were no other customers. The labels and price tags were all handwritten. The walls were lined with cork, and pinned to the cork were picture discs in plastic sleeves and dog-eared posters, faded where closest to the window.

"Can I help you?" asked the man behind the counter.

I checked to see if he had a face I knew. But as far as I could tell, he didn't. I don't think I'd ever known any men with a ponytail—not on principle, just that our paths had never crossed.

"Just looking," I said, and he nodded.

"If you need any help, just ask."

"Sure."

He nodded again, and began flicking through a magazine.

· · ·

I knew exactly what I was looking for. A catalyst from one of my earliest memories, from way back in childhood. Something I would have heard around the time I was learning to talk. As far back as memories go. Little Richard.

Now would that be under L or R, I wondered. Did "Little" count as a first name?

I guessed not, checked under L anyway, and found what I was looking for immediately. Oddly, also shelved under L were Chubby Checker and Fats Domino. But no matter, I'd found Little Richard's greatest hits.

I took my find back to the man at the counter.

"Actually," I said, "I could use some help. Could you play this for me?"

The man took a look at what I was holding.

"Which tune?"

I didn't need to look at the listing to know the answer. "'Good Golly Miss Molly.'"

In one movement, he slid out the LP, gave the vinyl an expert spin to flip the disc over, and dropped the record down onto the turntable.

"You got it."

He must have placed the needle just after the start of the track, because the music started so abruptly. And with it, Little Richard's distinctive singing voice.

"Good Golly Miss Molly. So like a mo. Good Golly Miss Molly. So like a mo. The way the rocking and a rolling. You can't get your mama home."

I felt a sudden lifting of my spirits. In exactly the way I had hoped, I felt transported by the sound. A wash of half-memories hit me—sitting on the floor, looking up at my dad, a tall and shadowy presence by the stereo, a machine which was mysterious to me and positioned beyond my reach, outside my line of sight.

The feeling of nostalgia was so strong I half expected to wake up there and then. And perhaps I might have, if something strange hadn't happened to the tune.

Although I couldn't really understand how, the passage of music that had been played seemed to loop directly and seamlessly back to the point where it had begun. No sooner had Little Richard completed his short chorus than he was singing it again.

"Good Golly Miss Molly. So like a mo. Good Golly Miss Molly. So like a mo. The way the rocking and a rolling. You can't get your mama home."

And now that I heard the chorus again, the lyrics didn't seem quite right. They sounded right, just didn't *seem* right.

When the chorus started to repeat for a third time, I gestured to the man to lift the needle.

"Heard enough?" he asked when the music stopped.

"Yes," I said—then corrected myself. "No. Is there something wrong with this record?"

The man frowned. "Wrong?"

"Is it stuck or . . ."

"Is it scratched?"

"Yes."

He seemed to take mild offense. "It's not scratched. I don't sell scratched records."

"Yes, but . . ."

"Can you hear the needle jumping?"

"No, but . . . it's repeating. I mean—the lyrics. There's more to the lyrics than that, isn't there?"

"Listen," said the man. "Don't play this song for the lyrics. It's Little Richard, not Leonard Cohen. If you don't like the lyrics, choose another record."

". . . Right," I said.

"And I happen to like the lyrics," he added, as I turned back to the shelves.

. . .

I started searching again. And now I realized, as I flicked through the albums, that although the records were stacked as if they had been alphabetized, they were certainly not. Under A, I found people whose names began with H. Under B, I found Schubert. Under C, nobody was there at all.

"I don't understand your system here," I called to the man.

"I do," he replied. "What are you looking for?"

I thought a moment. "The Beach Boys."

"Under P."

"P?"

"Or S."

". . . Why?"

"Pet Sounds."

Pet Sounds—perfect. This, more than Little Richard, was a soundtrack of childhood. This was after I had learned to talk, when I could choose a record for myself, and could stand on a chair to reach the stereo, and could place the needle without being supervised. And sing along.

. . .

"We sailed on the sloop John B. My grand-daddy and me. Show me the captain ashore, I want to go home. I want to go home, I want to go home. I feel so broke up. Let me go home."

So far, so good, I said to myself. So far, so . . .

"The first mate he got the shits. He ate up all of my grits. Call the captain ashore . . ."

Got the shits?

"Don't you want this?" called the man as I headed for the door.

"Time waster," as the door closed behind me with the chime of a bell.

I felt puzzled. I didn't quite know why these familiar songs were so elusive. I remained puzzled until I visited the bookshop on the other side of the road.

7.

The experience in the bookshop was worse. I walked up to the shop assistant with a stack of literature I had pulled from the shelves, and lifted the first book on the pile. "This is one of the greatest novels ever written," I said.

The girl examined the book jacket over the top of her glasses, then nodded her approval. "It's wonderful. A classic. I've read it three times."

"Three times? Really? How long did it take you?"

"Oh . . ." She looked surprised. "I don't know. I read it first on holiday, and . . . Maybe a week or so."

"A week? I just read the whole thing in less than a minute."

". . . A minute?"

"Do you want to know how?"

"Uh," she said, glancing around nervously, ". . . I suppose so."

"This is how." I began flicking through the pages. "Because the only sentence in this entire book is 'Call me Ishmael,' written a few hundred thousand times. Tell me—do you think that constitutes great literature?"

"It . . ."

"And how about this," I said, showing her the second book in the pile. "Another great novel you can plow through in under three seconds. 'It was the best of times, it was the worst of times.' Want to know what happens next?"

"I . . ."

"Tough. That's all there is. But no problem, we'll move on to *The Catcher in the Rye.*" I cleared my throat. "'Pretty phoney,' said Holden Caulfield. The end."

"Sir . . ." said the girl.

"Wait. I haven't got to Austen yet. 'It is a truth universally acknowledged that a man in want of a woman is a man in need of things that a woman with needs can want to universally acknowledge.'" I closed the book with a snap. "It goes on in a similar vein for another three-hundred-odd pages. It makes you wonder why they teach it at school, don't you think?"

"Sir," said the girl, "I'm going to have to ask you to leave."

8.

Outside the bookshop, I looked at the buildings opposite and I marveled at the absolute madness of my memory. On these buildings, I could see bricks. On the bricks, I could see variations in color from one brick to the next, and between the bricks I could see areas that needed repointing. I could see water stains beneath ledges and around gutters, and lead flashing beneath dormer windows. The windows were sash. In one pane, I could see that the glass was perfectly flat, whereas in the next pane I could see that the glass was subtly warping its reflection, and I knew that the flat glass was from a modern replacement following a break or crack, and the warped glass was original.

The road surface. Changes in the road surface, different kinds of tarmac, different shades of gray. Shapes of different tarmac—interlocking and overlapping rectangles. Strips, where the road surface had been dug up for work to the water main, or electricity lines, or gas supply. Different levels to the tarmac. Places where a pothole had been repaired. Places where a pothole had not yet been repaired.

The pavement, marked with grease and rain and chewing gum. Thousands of pieces of discarded chewing gum, pressed flat by pedestrians into a constellation. And if I reached down to touch the pavement, I could feel grit beneath my fingers. The grit stuck to the natural oils on my hand. If I lifted my hand and looked at the grit, I could see that like grubby snowflakes each grain was different from the others.

Detail. Spectacular. Fractal. The threads that constructed my shirt, and the smaller threads that constructed the larger threads. The shapes of the clouds above, the shapes that led to further shapes, and the slow movement of the clouds across the sky. The cloud shadows that passed across the tarmac and softened the brightness of the closed windows. An open window, through which I could dimly make out the patterned wallpaper inside.

Spectacular, fractal, *awesome* detail of the way the world looked. Presented by my memory effortlessly, with no act of concentration. No pause to assemble or consider the image as my gaze swept from left to right, or up or down, or anywhere.

And yet. Call on my memory to remember a handful of words from a familiar song, and it tripped, and it fell.

Now, surrounded by this impressive and useless detail, I considered for a moment that waking from the coma was going to be more difficult than I had first imagined. I suppose that my initial realization—that I was dreaming—had made the coma seem more domestic and less dramatic than it really was. After all, up to this point in my life, all I had ever done was wake from dreams. Waking was the most reliable part of a dream, as built into dreams as death is to life.

You dream, you wake: you live, you die.

Somehow, it occurred to me that if you die, you wake.

From the top of one of the tall buildings I had been examining, I stood on the coping stones that bordered the flat roof. This was a red-brick mansion block with shops at street level that sold empty books and fractured records. There were eight stories between me and the chewing gum and the pavement.

I held my arms slightly away from my body and stretched my fingers out like the feathers at the end of a hawk's wing. Although I had no aerodynamic expectations of my fingers. The purpose here was not to fly.

Looking down, courage deserted and found me by turns, and rocked me gently on the soles of my shoes. The courage always seemed at odds with the wind you find at high places. When the courage was with me, the wind pushed me away from the ledge, catching my shirt, ballooning the material around my back. When my courage was failing, the wind pushed me from behind, towards the drop, pressing my shirt flat.

I shut my eyes. I listened to the sound of the wind. Through the sound of the wind, I heard a diesel engine.

The next time the wind blew, I allowed myself to step in that direction.

9.

"You again."

I opened my eyes and found myself gazing into someone else's. In a rearview mirror, the eyes of the cabbie who had driven me back from the hospital.

"Yes," I said. "Me again."

"What are the chances of that happening? Picking you up twice."

"Surprisingly high," I said, relaxing into the back seat. "I must have stepped backwards."

"Excuse me?"

"I said, I must have stepped backwards. From the roof."

"What roof?"

"I nearly just jumped off the top of a building."

"Life getting you down?"

"No."

"What stopped you from jumping?"

"I don't know. The wind wasn't with me."

The cabbie's curiosity seemed to have passed. "So, where are we going?" he asked, businesslike.

I thought for a moment. "I'll get back to you on that," I said.

So passages from favorite pieces of music or literature were too incomplete to provide the waking trigger I was looking for. And if my encounters with Anthony or Mary or Catherine were anything to go by, then conversations with dream people were not going to do the trick either.

But if my memory could be relied upon to produce buildings with accuracy, then perhaps I still had an ace up my sleeve. Some buildings, or locations, were as evocative as music or conversations. And buildings could be explored. Rooms could lead to corridors that led to further rooms.

It was a question of finding the right building.

"Do you know where I went to school?" I said.

"I couldn't guess," the cabbie replied. "Give me a clue."

I shook my head. "It's not a guessing game. I'm asking you if you happen to know where I went to school."

"Would I know a thing like that?"

"I just thought perhaps you might."

He craned around in his seat to shoot me an incredulous look. "I'd have thought *you* might."

"Yes," I agreed. "But I don't."

"So, is it your old school you're after?"

"Not necessarily. It was just the first place that came to mind. What I'm after is . . ." I paused. "A trip down memory lane."

"Memory Lane . . . is that south of the river?"

"I was using a figure of speech."

"And I was making a joke."

When it became apparent that I wasn't about to laugh, the cabbie cleared his throat. "If I was after a trip down memory lane, I'd want to go back to the house where I grew up."

"Ah. That would be ideal."

"So why don't we head there?"

"I'd love to."

I didn't add anything more, such as the street address the cabbie was doubtless expecting.

Eventually, he said, "You don't know where that is either."

"No," I said.

"So how do you expect us to find it?"

"I suppose . . ."

I suppose I was hoping that by mentioning the house I grew up in, or my old school, we would simply find ourselves there. It had happened that way with the hospital, and the record shop, and standing on the roof. Up to now, the relocations had been quite easy. Even helpful. But perhaps not anymore.

". . . I was hoping for the best," I finished.

"I think you have to do more than hope," said the cabbie, and I wondered if he was chiding me.

"What do you suggest?"

"Well, I'm a cab driver. I drive around everywhere. Chances are, I've driven past the house where you grew up on more than one occasion. I've probably dropped off on that street. I probably know it well."

"Okay . . ."

"If you could manage to describe something about the house or the area, there's a good chance you might be able to tell me more than you think."

"Describe the house . . ."

Yes—a sensible enough suggestion. But hopelessly let down by my amnesia, which at the moment was permitting me only the snapshot I had seen in the record shop—of a child's perspective of a shadow father figure standing by a turntable that was out of sight.

The cabbie was waiting. I felt too embarrassed to say I couldn't tell him anything useful, so I winged it.

"The house had a roof," I said, then added, "obviously," to show I was only getting started.

"Roof," the cabbie noted seriously.

"And a front door. Walls and what have you."

"Roof, front door, walls. With you so far."

I tried to think of other features my house was likely to have had. I didn't want to mislead him with false information, but I wasn't sure what else I could confidently suggest.

"Windows?" the cabbie prompted.

"Yes," I said quickly. "Several."

"A front garden?"

A front garden.

I had a sudden flash, a sense of place. A sense of movement, backwards and forwards. Then falling.

". . . A swing. Of course."

"What?"

"A small front garden, with a tree and a swing."

"Ah. So now we're getting somewhere. Do you know how many houses have a front garden and a tree?"

"I don't."

"Fewer than most. So I think your house will be found in one of the more comfortable parts of town."

I nodded. "I don't recall discomfort."

"There," said the cabbie. "And I'll tell you another thing. I would hazard a guess that the house was built after cars became commonplace. Because in the older houses, where the streets were widened, the front gardens disappeared. No—you grew up in a suburb."

"You're very good," I said.

The cabbie's eyes sparkled again. "I can picture the place already."

"Yes," I said. "So can I."

10.

It was clear that nobody had lived in the house for quite some time, because the grass in the front garden was meadowlike, and the windows were black and framed with peeling paint, and the net curtains inside were gray and torn. So my parents, or my dream parents, whose faces I couldn't picture and whose names I couldn't place, were either dead or had moved on long ago.

It was also clear that this was a dream house. The dilapidation was not a memory but a representation of a poorly remembered past. It was a metaphor I could walk around in and clear metaphorical cobwebs from.

And it was also, for these reasons, a disappointment: that this rather obvious representation of a poorly remembered past was the best I could do.

Long grass and black windows. A bit of rope hanging
from a tree that once held the swing, whose wooden
board had rotted away. A front path, where moss grew
over broken concrete and dandelions pushed through
the cracks.

But never mind. This was the house I'd grown up
in, so at least I was in the right place. And little details
about the house were coming back to me fast. I knew
that when I pushed open the front door, it would give
a low bass creak, from the wood rather than the hinges,
and I knew that as I stepped through, loose hall tiles
would click as I walked across them.

"Remember what I told you," the cabbie called
through the driver's window.

"Remember what?" I called back.

"About taking things slowly."

"Okay," I said.

Behind me, the cab's diesel engine started up, then
faded.

11.

The wood did creak, the tiles did click, and there was further familiarity in the hallway's cool and settled air, and the sound of the front door closing behind me.

There was something else too. It was subtle. It was a slight lift away from the floor I stood on, as if I had become lighter. It was the feeling after you've put down a heavy bag you've been carrying for a while, that your shoulders are drifting towards the ceiling.

And—it was a shift within myself. In the fabric of myself, as if, relative to the house and the hallway, I was occupying less of the space than I should. I lifted my hand to inspect it, and expected to see through my fingers as though my flesh and bones were cloudy glass. Instead, I simply saw my hand. But the feeling remained. Whether I was or wasn't, I *felt* translucent.

I would say it took me several seconds to recognize these sensations for what they were—but dream life was not structured according to seconds or minutes. Instead I could say that several moments passed, or just that something passed, until I realized: this exercise, this return to the house in which I grew up, was going to work. In the house, I would wake.

In fact, I *was* waking.

The thought gave me pause. It made me catch my breath. Somehow I knew, or felt sure, the waking process would be fragile, as delicate a process as falling asleep. It was something I could get wrong. A sudden sound, anything that jarred or surprised, and the opportunity would be gone.

So as the cabbie had instructed, I slowed myself down and looked around. From my position in the hallway, I had a choice. I could climb the stairs or continue across the clicking tiles towards the kitchen and the living room.

In the living room, I'd find the stereo. I remembered how powerful the effect of listening to Little Richard had been in the record shop, before the song began to fracture and loop. It seemed to me that if I were to listen to "Miss Molly" here, the effect would be that much more powerful.

But it also seemed to me that the stairs were exerting a kind of gravity, pulling me in their direction. I wondered if I was tracking a particular memory, and if there was a route I had to follow through the house. The memory might be dependent on sticking to the route, and waking might be dependent on completing the memory.

I turned the choices over and decided I should go with gravity, which I assumed to be the working of my instincts. So I climbed the stairs and forced myself to be unhurried, and as I climbed I noticed that the lightness and the sense of translucence remained. Maybe even grew a little stronger as I ascended. This made me confident that if there was a route to follow, I was on it.

At the top of the stairs I stopped again, now on the landing, looking for another gravity tug to lead me. Here, I could walk straight ahead to the family bathroom. Or, to the left, down the corridor, was my parents' bedroom, which overlooked the street. And to the right was my bedroom.

While I waited for an indication of which direction to take, I noticed that the dilapidation I had seen on the outside of the building did not extend to the inside. The house was quiet and somewhat lifeless, but in good shape. The brown carpet on the landing wasn't frayed, the wallpaper wasn't stained or hanging damply off the plaster.

It was, however, dark compared to the bright day outside. Ambient light filtered under the closed doors off the landing and from the hallway below, but I couldn't see as well as I would have liked. I still had the slight blindness that follows the sudden movement from light to dark, and my eyes seemed unwilling or unable to adjust.

I continued waiting. It finally occurred to me that the reason I wasn't being pulled in any particular direction was because I was in the right place for the memory to begin.

12.

"*Hello, Carl.*"

The door to my parents' bedroom had opened, and the landing was filled with light, and now my unadjusted eyes were blinded by the brightness rather than the gloom.

"*How are you doing today?*"

In the doorway was the tall silhouette I had recollected in the record shop. It was my dad, backlit, stooping down to look at me while I blinked and squinted against the glare.

Then he was walking in my direction, right at me it seemed, a looming shadow—and I thought we were going to collide and he would send me falling backwards down the stairs. But simultaneously, something was happening to the perspective of the shadow—it was looming unnaturally large, unnaturally fast. And

at the moment I expected and braced for the colli-
sion, and my dad's shadow swamped even my peripheral vision in blackness—he simply passed right
through me.

I made sense of it moments later. He hadn't walked
through me, he had walked over me. That is how large
he was, and how small I was.

I turned quickly, just in time to see his figure reach
the bottom of the stairs. Then he had doubled back
around, and was walking down the hallway towards
the living room. Frustratingly, if it hadn't been for my
angled viewpoint at the top of the stairs, I might have
been able to see him clearly. But instead I saw him only
as a moving shape, a zoetrope between the banisters.

13.

I followed him of course. I had confidence now. A good deal of confidence about the way this would play out, and why it would play out that way. Confidence in my whole approach to having discovered I was still in a coma. A degree of self-congratulation that I hadn't panicked, too much. Self-congratulation that I had been calm and thoughtful, and had thought and planned my way out of what was, in truth and in all senses, a mess.

It had all worked out like this:

I'm attacked.

I fall unconscious.

I think I wake.

The world is fractured and weird.

I think I'm traumatized.

I think I'm brain damaged.

I realize I am neither, I'm in a coma.

I realize I have to wake.

So I plan.

I look for a catalyst, and I find a fragment of a memory, in the form of "Miss Molly."

By searching, and by coaxing, I find more frag-
ments.

Gardens, swings, bricks, and windows.

They lead me to the house where I grew up.

Where the "Miss Molly" memory is placed in
context.

Where I become light and weightless.

And the memory becomes as complete.

As complete as it needs to be.

And—perhaps this is where I congratulate myself the
most—I do all this alone. I do all this alone; everything
I achieve, I achieve alone, because it's my head I'm locked
into, and I share this space with nobody but myself.

In the living room, I saw my dad. Standing beside him
was my mother. Still silhouettes, now against the French
windows to the back garden. But I didn't need to see
their faces to know them.

I was unable to speak. The fabric of my body was
now as weightless as a single spider web.

They both turned to look at me.

Then my father said, *"This one bothers me a lot."*

And my mother said, *"More than the others?"*

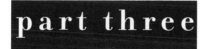

part three

1.

Waking is rising: You wake up, not down.

Waking is rising, which is why my shoulders were drifting as I walked into the house. At that point I was like a diver on the bottom of the ocean, discarding lead weights. And when I saw the shadows of my mother and father, the final lead belt was released and I began a quick upward trajectory.

It was only as I started to rise that I realized how cold and dark the water was at the bottom of the ocean, and how badly my lungs were aching to take a breath, and how keen I was to leave the bottom of the ocean behind.

The trajectory felt one-way. The rising was helpless and inevitable. I felt sure that nothing could return me to the place I was leaving. I was passing through thermoclimes, and the water was warming and becoming brighter. I was moving towards splintered light.

I remembered a few things about waking.

I remembered the sense of surprise as dream life and waking life swapped primacy, and the way in which the most tangible and deeply involving dreams could bleach entirely away. I remembered that waking life *had* primacy, that the dreamed horror of losing your family was nothing to the reality of a pillow at the back of your head.

I remembered things that made waking life so different from dream life. The crystal qualities, the sense that the world existed in three hundred and sixty degrees rather than in narrow bands of vision. I remembered that waking was a hundred different kinds of clarities, and I braced for them to come as a cascade.

In anticipation of the clarities, it was already hard to believe that dream life had ever seemed so real.

Then, just as my fingers, the outstretched fingers of my outstretched arm, were about to break through . . .

Just as I was about to *wake,* something closed around my ankle and stopped my ascent. It held me in the warm water, at the boundary of full consciousness, so close to air and daylight that I could see shapes behind the water's distorting surface.

I blinked and tried to focus, and saw two figures. They weren't my parents at all.

2.

"*This one bothers me a lot.*"
  "*More than the others?*"
  "*More than the others. Yes.*"
  "*Why?*"

Two people stood beside me.

  A man. The nurse. I recognized his voice.

  A woman. A doctor, perhaps. She had asked why I bothered the nurse more than the others, but she sounded distracted, uninterested in the answer.

  They weren't looking at me. They were looking at a clipboard.

  I looked up. I felt as if I were in a frame. I could see metal bars that were vertical, and others that were horizontal.

I looked down and saw that something was covering my nose and mouth. A ventilator. It seemed to be both muffling and amplifying my breathing.

I tried to move my hand. I couldn't tell if anything happened.

"The lack of movement," said the nurse.

The doctor moved away. Towards an area of brightness, maybe a window, maybe the door of the room. Either way, out of my sight.

But I could still hear her voice.

"Well," she said. "We won't know for certain unless he wakes."

3.

If my eyes really had been open—and for a few seconds I really had been looking at the interior of my ward room—I now closed them.

Waking is rising, and dreaming is sinking. You wake up, you fall asleep.

I began sinking back into my dream.

It's possible that the nurse and the doctor were talking in a way that was careless or irresponsible, that they had forgotten the presence of the comatose in the way that people can forget the presence of cameras. But I don't think so. I think the nurse was talking to me, directly and deliberately. I knew of at least one instance in which he had done this before, when he had asked me to squeeze his hand. And there were earlier instances when he had been a presence in my dream, which I imagine was a result of his bedside presence. And now he had orchestrated a conversation with a doctor because it was a conversation he wanted me to overhear.

I had been sent a telegraph, a headline piece of information: that there was a choice to be made, between the uncertainties of the dream world and the uncertainties of the waking world.

So I didn't kick to keep from sinking, or struggle or fight. But I did feel some despair, that overcoming one strange and desperate situation had only left me in another. And I did feel frightened, that uncertainty was the only prize on offer. And I imagine that is why the dream world I returned to was so different from the dream world I had left.

4.

I sank and I sank, and when I reopened my eyes, I was in total darkness. So I assumed I was still sinking, or descending, and I simply had to wait until I reached the plane on which the dream landscape would reestablish itself.

An amount of time passed—long enough for me to realize that either I was descending at a slower rate than I had risen or I was descending to a far deeper plane than my previous landscape. Then more time passed, and I began to wonder if perhaps I wasn't actually descending anymore. Perhaps I had already arrived at whatever place I had been descending to, and was now motionless.

With nothing to see in the total darkness, I had to rely on touch. But a cautious sweep of my arms told me there was nothing immediately within reach of my hands. Then an equally cautious step told me that there was nothing in reach of my feet either. In fact, I didn't seem to be standing on anything. Meaning, I supposed, that wherever I was, I was suspended.

But suspended in what? While rising, I'd had the sensation of moving upwards through water. I wasn't in water now. When I moved my arms or legs, or turned my head, I felt no resistance. And when I moved my arms more violently, fast and hard enough to have felt the resistance of air, I still felt nothing.

I took a pause. To try to think. But I didn't get a chance to think, because during the pause, I noticed that besides feeling nothing at the ends of my limbs, and seeing nothing, I could also hear nothing. Not the sound of my breathing, or the rustle of my clothes, or the sound of any other person or entity or machine or object that shared this space with me.

So I tried to speak, and I made no sound.

And I tried to clap my hands, but when I swung my hands together, my palms made no contact. Nor was the swinging of my hands something I could feel sure I had actually done. None of my movements were evidenced by any sensation whatsoever. I couldn't feel the parting of my lips or the blinking of my eyes.

Finally, I reached up to touch my face, and there simply wasn't anything there. My fingers moved into emptiness, continuing backwards through what should have been a skull, and beyond, until the movement became impossible, requiring a dislocation of arms and shoulder sockets that I clearly didn't have. At which point, I lost track of any understanding of what movements might be, and how the now nonexistent parts of my body might have previously related to one another. I lost track of any understanding of physicality at all.

I was conscious, and that's all. Beyond my consciousness, there wasn't anything else.

More time passed. I waited for something to happen. Nothing happened.

I was calm. Or frozen. I felt as if I was on the verge of having the most terrifying thought in the world, but I wasn't having it quite yet.

Then I had it.

5·

Is this what I am?

It doesn't sound so terrifying, spelled out like that. Maybe you had to be there . . .

In any case, the thought was: Is this what I am?

As in, if I were to lose an arm in an accident, I'd still be me. Nobody would say I wasn't me. They wouldn't say, He used to be Carl, then he lost an arm, and now he's John.

And if, in another accident, I lost the other arm, the same would be true. Likewise with my legs, my sight, my hearing, my speech, my sense of touch. You could keep going, keep stripping me down, until I was only a consciousness, suspended in a void.

But take away the consciousness, and suddenly I'm gone. Carl is no more. And take away the consciousness but leave the body, leave the full complement of arms and legs, and I'm still gone.

So: whether dreaming or waking, this is what I am.

Whether dreaming *or* waking, *this* is what I am?

This?

From that point, it was only a hop, skip, and a

jump to the lonely meaninglessness of everything. And
having already lost my body, I now lost my mind.

As a consciousness in a void, losing your mind is serious,
given that a mind is all you are. Unlike losing your mind
in the context of waking life, nothing external is going
to assert itself as a counterpoint to your breakdown. You
aren't going to find or be provided with any anchors.

That said, "losing your mind" is a figure of speech,
and it's misleading in this context. If you are a mind in a
void and you lose your mind, it implies that your mind
is misplaced, somewhere else, which leaves you only as
a void. Something blank. But that's not what happened, because obviously I still *had* my mind; it just
wasn't functioning. And actually, I was the opposite of
blank—I was full up, or overly full, and bursting.

The surprise for me is that I can remember exactly
what losing my mind was like. It's tangible to me; it's
a taste in my mouth. And, even more surprisingly, I
think I'm able to describe it.

Imagine a tone of voice. The tone is sort of dreary.
But it's also despairing and frustrated. If the tone was
matched to a voice, it would be the nasal voice of a boring man, intoning his despair weakly: *Oh no, no, God, oh*

dear, oh no . . . But forget about what the voice is saying—it's the tone that's important. Dreary, despairing,
frustrated, pathetic, and quite loud. So take that loud
tone and make it ingredient number one.

Second ingredient, very straightforward: fear. Jit-
tery, panicky. Something that you wouldn't think would
coexist with the dreary tone, but does. Quivering, cold,
biting fear.

The third and final ingredient, also straightforward: random words. Random words, strung together.
Strings of words. Simple and unhinged. Without pat-
tern, no looping, no meaningful repetitions. And
SHOUTED AT TOP VOLUME.

BENT UNION TRACK OVER FINE CUBA ORE
UNDER RED SORT ETHER INK TOKE INTRO
SATURN NILE OR TRAP AMPS SECT REVS AVE
NET DRILL OFF MINT AMOK SATURN IND
TIMED FELL IS REP SEVER TALLOW SAP EASE
EVENT MET SAW

Crash these things together, make them exist to the
exclusion of everything else, and that's it.

6.

There are two things that puzzle me now. One is, how long did I stay in that insensible state? Obviously, it wasn't indefinite or I wouldn't be here now. But neither was it a short period of time. Somehow, I know that. It wasn't the equivalent of an alarm waking you at eight, then you slip back to sleep and have what feels like a long dream, then wake again to find that only ten minutes have passed.

If I were to make a guess, while taking into account the odd time-keeping qualities of internal life, I'd say I was adrift for perhaps two or three months of waking life. But a guess is all it is.

The second thing that puzzles me is: What pulled me out? Given the void, the absence of anchors, why *didn't* the mind loss continue indefinitely?

That I really have no answer to, and no guess either. All I know is, quite abruptly, like a tap being turned off, the madness stopped and I was shunted back into the more familiar dream landscape I had been inhabiting before.

It felt like home.

It was home. It was my bed, and I was with Catherine. And she had her arms around me, and she was saying, "Hey, don't worry. It's okay. It's okay." Then she was kissing me and saying that she loved me. And her lips were soft and warm, and I could smell her, and it all felt completely real.

And I although I was confused, punch-drunk, mentally beaten up, my presence of mind—my lost mind—began returning to me amazingly fast.

And I knew this was still a dream, and this wasn't really my bed, and Catherine wasn't really there, and didn't really love me. But, crucially, I didn't care.

7.

That morning, this is what we did. We made love, we took a shower, then we went downstairs and had breakfast.

None of it was real. I didn't care.

For breakfast I ate bacon and toast.

It wasn't real bacon, and I didn't care.

A couple of times, something weird happened. For example, the bacon and toast took literally no time to cook, they just appeared. And the kitchen was maybe two times narrower than its real-life counterpart, with higher ceilings.

But I didn't care.

Because why would I? Strip down my waking life, and I'm a consciousness in a void. Strip down my dream life, and I'm a consciousness in a void.

What difference?

After breakfast, we went for a walk.

8.

At the end of my street, we turned right on to the main road that led down to the river. It was mid-morning and the day was shaping up to be hot. Catherine was wearing a sun hat and a pretty summer dress, cotton, flower patterned. I was wearing jeans and a short-sleeved shirt, and I carried a small backpack with a water bottle inside and a camera.

Rather than walk the length of the main road in the growing heat and tire ourselves out, we chose to take the pedestrian subway, which had recently been extended. One could now travel the full distance to the river in air-conditioning, away from the traffic noise and exhaust fumes. One could even do a little shopping en route. Several outlets had opened up in the small alcoves that lined the walkway, most of them selling clothes and jewelry. It made the journey a little longer and a little slower than it might otherwise have been, because Catherine kept pausing to check the wares. I would be chatting away, in mid-sentence, and turn to look at her, only to realize that for the last few paces I had been talking to myself.

The pedestrian subway was also a little disorienting, because it was hard to judge how far one had traveled. Periodically there were staircases back to street level, but by some strange oversight, they had not yet been signposted to mark at which cross streets they exited. So we ended up guessing which exit to take and, by chance, chose the right one.

We came out at the bridge, where we paused to take a drink from the water bottle. We had been underground for perhaps half an hour, but already the day had got a good deal hotter. Either that or we had been softened by the air-conditioning. I began to wish I'd had Catherine's good sense and brought a cap along, because I could tell that in this weather I was likely to burn.

"Where do you want to go?" I asked Catherine.

Catherine shrugged. She was leaning on the guardrail of the bridge, looking down at the slow-moving water below. "Do you think they eat their catch?" she said, indicating the fishermen who were sitting on the sloped concrete banks. "The river always looks so dirty."

"I don't think they do," I said. "I think there may be a rule about having to put the catch back."

But I wasn't sure. A little way down the river, the banks were crowded with the wooden shacks and shanties where many of these fishermen lived. A different part of town, less affluent. Looking at their homes, it suddenly seemed unlikely they spent their days idly fishing for sport.

"I think they do eat them," Catherine said, maybe having followed the same thought process as me. "I bet they taste of mud."

"The fishermen or the fish?"

"Both." She stood up from the guardrail. "How about we head through the antique district and then up to one of the shrines?"

Now it was me who stopped at every shop window and Catherine who hovered impatiently ahead. I was distracted mainly by the small carved bone and ivory figurines that were for sale in most of the shops. The good ones were all far too expensive to buy, but I enjoyed looking at them, and I liked the smell of incense that floated out from the doorways.

One figurine caught my eye. It was an old man, squatting, with one hand resting on his knee and the other holding a fan. His head was angled, and he was looking straight up at me. He had an odd expression— a kind of grimace, slightly disapproving, but also angrily amused.

Beside the old man was another figurine, this one standing. It seemed even older than the rest, but it wasn't ivory or bone. It looked as if it was made from clay or porcelain, and I wondered if this meant it would be more affordable than the others. The years had beaten it up a little. The glaze was cracked and chipped, and all of its protuberances—the folds of its clothes, its feet and hands—were worn down as if it had spent years knocking around inside someone's pocket.

Examining it more closely, I saw that although the figurine was proportioned like a man and wearing clothes, a robe, its face was oddly pointed. Not a human face. There was a snout, doglike, but less pronounced.

As I looked at the curious face, a hand inside the shop picked it up. The shopkeeper, who looked not unlike the squatting old man I had been examining before, was gazing at me with the same odd grimace.

He held the standing figurine up to the window for me to see, then gave it a little flick on the back. And the dog face stuck its tongue out at me.

The shopkeeper's grimace changed into a grin. This was his little trick to surprise customers. He did it a couple more times, and I saw that the tongue was loose in the head, a small sliver of bone. Its natural resting position was inside, but when the back was tapped, out it came.

The shopkeeper said something but I missed it. I cupped a hand to my ear.

"Monkey God!" I heard faintly through the glass.

"Having fun?" asked Catherine, appearing beside me.

"I thought it was a dog," I said.

The shopkeeper did the trick again, pleased to have doubled his audience.

We ate lunch in a cheap restaurant that Catherine knew. She said it had to be cheap, given that we had left the antique district with the porcelain Monkey God in my pocket, loosely bound in bubble wrap. It turned out to be not less expensive than the ivory figures, but more. But I wasn't overly worried at the cost. In fact, the cost was the point. I think I wanted Catherine's scandalized reaction to my extravagance more than I wanted the figurine itself.

Catherine wanted to wait until the late afternoon, so the heat didn't tire us out as we walked around the grounds of the shrine she wanted to visit, which she had described as her favorite in the city. So we let lunch drag on a while. We drank tea, and let the waitress keep refilling the cups, and left the bill unpaid on the table until the shadows of the passersby were just starting to lengthen.

9.

We explored the shrine and temple complex for hours. First, the cool interior, where the floorboards made a singsong creak as you walked over them, in a way that made you think of birdsong. Then the gardens, which were full of secret areas, and quiet streams and ponds.

10.

We ended up eating ice cream, sitting on stone steps beneath the canopy of a huge maple tree growing near the main entrance.

"So, you haven't yet told me," I said, "why this is your favorite shrine."

"Well," Catherine replied, "it has a very dramatic front door." She pointed with the little shovel spoon that had been tucked into the ice cream lid. The front doors—or gates, to be more accurate—were indeed dramatic, and famous for their size. A feat of ancient engineering: they were more than twice the height of any of the surrounding buildings, modern or old. A tourist attraction: on the street side of the gates, there was a booth where you could have your photo taken with a camera with a distorted lens, so that both you and the full size of the gates were included in the frame.

Sometimes after getting the photo, the tourists would leave without bothering to visit the shrine behind.

"But also, it's very peaceful," Catherine continued.

I nodded. "I can't hear any traffic. Just . . ."

"Floorboards."

I laughed. "Yes. What's that about, the floorboards?"

"They were built that way. The iron nails are driven into the wood at an angle, or something like that. The idea was that if a thief arrived during the night, the noise would alert everyone to their presence."

"A burglar alarm."

"Uh-huh."

"You know a lot about this place."

"As I said, it's my favorite."

"You've been here often."

Catherine paused. "Actually, no. This is only my second time."

A group of young monks walked by. I noticed as they passed that the sky was turning the same color as their robes. The sun, which was out of sight behind the tall gates, was either close to or on the horizon line.

I ate the last spoonful of my ice cream.

"You know what?" I said, putting down the empty carton. "This was a perfect day."

"Yes," said Catherine. "It was a good day."

"A perfect day," I repeated, thinking back to our morning in bed, and late breakfast, and the general way in which our time together had unfolded. "I can't imagine what else I'd want in the hours of daylight."

"Uh-huh. It . . ."

She stopped. Her voice had caught.

"It . . . ?" I prompted.

"It was good."

"You've had a better day than this?"

Catherine didn't reply.

"You won the lottery, and found a Caravaggio that someone had tossed into your back garden."

I glanced at her, expecting something: a smile, or at least a half-smile. But instead she suddenly looked rather sad. I felt confused. I could tell that there had been a shift in the atmosphere, but I couldn't see the reason for the shift.

"The first time I came here," Catherine said eventually. "That was better."

"Why?" I said, and immediately tried to retract. "No," I began. "You don't have to—"

But she cut in. "I was with someone else."

"Right," I said. Then repeated it. "Right."

I sounded pretty stupid. Clumsy. I suppose I just wanted to make it sound like we were still having a normal, unloaded conversation. Which was a waste of time, because a couple of seconds later I loaded it up again by asking, "Who?"

"It doesn't matter who," she replied. "That's the point."

I frowned. I wondered whether she was being deliberately provocative—weighting her lines to cause maximum unsettling effect. But in the way she returned my gaze, I could see that, in truth, she was doing the opposite. Her expression was regretful, and affectionate.

"What I'm saying, Carl, is that a good day only becomes a perfect day if you can share it with someone else."

"Oh," I said, as the penny dropped. "I see."

Then the garden and Catherine and everything were drowned out by a sudden flood of words. Similar to the *shouted word strings* I had heard before . . .

11.

In nirvana come and settle eden yet orca understood ardent rapture every infernal new talent earns rare endless summer towards eventual delight THE HIDDEN ENDING WOODEN ALLEGORIES LEFT KENNELED WITH AFFECTIONATE SAVAGE TO HEED REGENERATION OF UNSTRUCTURED GARDEN HAVING TAUGHT HASTE EVEN CERTAINTY IS TRUSTING YOU OR FORTUNE KICKED YOUR ORIGINS TO OTHERS.

. . . But oddly, although the words seemed less random than before, I think they had less meaning.

.   .   .

It can be hard to figure out what has meaning and what doesn't.

On the floor of my bathroom, the blood and bandages had dried into a solid mass. They cracked as I tried to lift them. Desiccated, they crumbled in my hands into black dust and fibers.

Through the window of their kitchen, I watched Mary position Joshua in a high chair as Anthony stood by the sink, looking out over his front garden. I was standing directly in his line of sight, but he was gazing right through me. Looking back at him, I decided I had never known him, or his wife, or their little son. Their faces were generic, their features anonymous. They seemed more like the mannequins of a window display than a family.

From the back seat of the cab, I decided that the eyes in the rearview mirror were the eyes of a friend. Older eyes than mine, belonging to someone I had trusted and felt guided by. I didn't know who the friend was. I did know they were real, and important enough to me that this sliver of face could muscle through my amnesia. But when I tried to maneuver in my position on the seat, to see a little more of the face, the reflection in the mirror remained unchanged.

I caught the smell of milk, warming in morning sunshine. From the radio in the milk float cabin, an indistinct tune was looping through a fuzz of static.

I tapped the back of the Monkey God, and the tongue popped out.

The curtains blew open.

All these relocations came fast. The transitions between them felt seamless. They were, I suppose, me thinking.

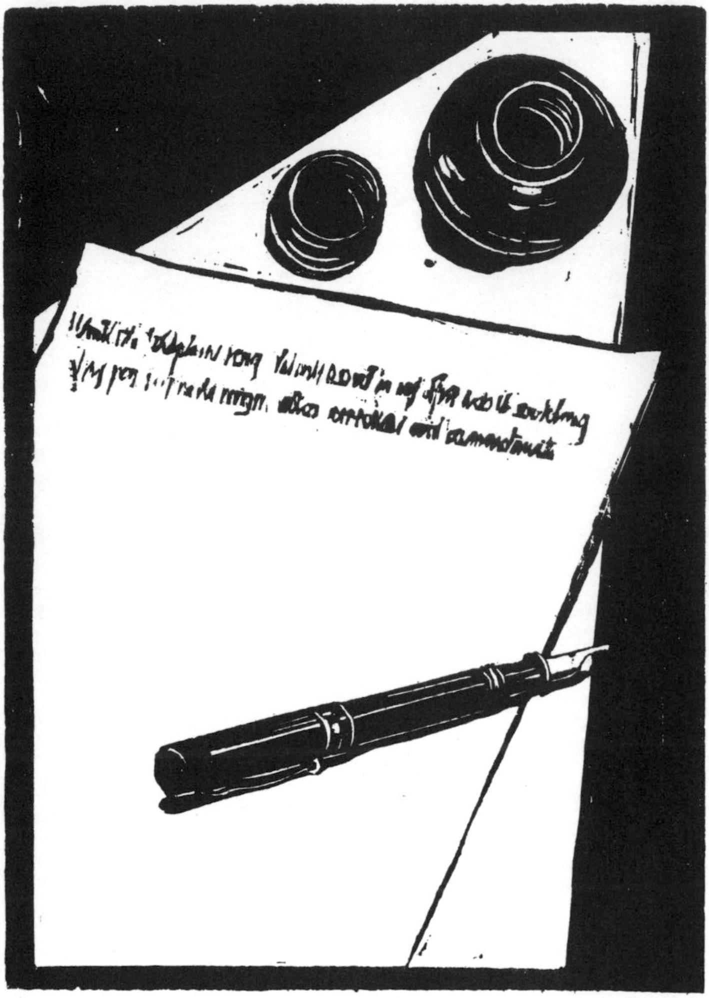

12.

In the final relocation, everything darkened rather quickly, in the same unexpected way as when a cloud passes over the sun. But the drop in light was closer to a moonless night. I felt a lurch of anxiety, fearing I might be about to be returned to the darkness of the void.

I put my hands out. If I had an object, or sensation, to hold on to, I could keep that place at bay.

I found, at the point of my elbow, at each arm, a curving shape.

That reassured me. Cautiously, I leaned backwards, and felt something that was both soft and firm, and sculpted for lumbar support.

I gave out a little sigh of relief. I wasn't floating in a lonely void. I was sitting on a chair in my office.

. . .

I reached over and switched on the desk lamp. Then I took a sheet of paper from the drawer on the left and a fountain pen from the drawer on the right, and I wrote:

Until the telephone rang, the only sound in my office was the scratching of my pen as I made margin notes, corrections, and amendments.

I pressed the speaker button.

"Carl speaking."

"Carl."

"Catherine! I meant to send you home hours ago—"

She interrupted me. "I am at home. I've been home, been out to see a film, eaten a pizza, paid the baby-sitter, and watched the end of *Newsnight.*"

The clock on my desk read 11:42. I turned in my chair. The window of my office was floor to ceiling. Through the window, I could see the city glitter and the night sky. No stars—a low cloud layer made the sky glow almost red.

Catherine continued. "I'm calling because the last train leaves in twenty-five minutes."

"Right," I said.

I hung up.

"Right."

I lifted my legs and braced my feet against the side of my desk. Then I kicked backwards as hard as I could.

13.

I flew across the floor, smashed through the window, and launched into space.

For a while, the shards of broken glass kept pace with me as I fell down the side of the office building. Then I, and the glass, and the chair lost touch with one another, like skydivers breaking formation.

Though I was falling fast, I was tumbling slowly. Initially I was facing the heavens with my back to the ground. But the weight of my upper body rotated me until I was looking at the city upside down. The strange perspective kept me unaware of the speed at which I was plummeting, and the same was true when I looked directly down at the ground. It was getting closer, but not as quickly as I might have expected. I had time to make out the movement of cars from their pinprick headlights.

The speed became apparent only when momentum had rotated me almost full circle and I was facing the building again and watching the stories flash by. Suddenly, the descent seemed immensely fast. Adrenaline and exhilaration snatched at my heart and made me suck in a breath—and as I did so, wind noise abruptly kicked in, as if the gasp had repressurized my eardrums.

And now I began to see static images through the lit windows that rushed past, only a couple of feet in front of my face. An effect grabbed me. It became the building that was moving, and me that was static. Like watching a train pass while standing on a platform.

14.

On the other side of the windows of the train, I saw two things.

The first was an advertisement, running above the windows. A photograph showed Anthony, smiling brightly, and behind him his bland family. The advertisement read: *Fresh milk, fresh coffee. Some things are just meant for each other.* I wasn't sure which of the two products he was selling, but I was glad to finally make sense of him.

The second thing I saw was the four young men, getting ready to move into the next carriage, where they would intimidate the girl who was reading her book, and shortly afterwards, attack me.

I call them young men, maybe because it makes me more comfortable about the ease with which they kicked me into oblivion, but in truth they were boys. The youngest was no older than fifteen. The oldest was possibly eighteen or nineteen. No shame, I suppose, in being beaten up by four teenagers—but still, it bothered me. Not as a physical thing, not as a comparison of speed and strength: as a disempowerment.

I wondered, as I looked at them through the grubby glass, if I would hear myself as I protested at the first moment of their attack. I had a horrible feeling that I would hear the same despairing tone I had half heard during the mind loss. A boring man, despairing weakly. *This is what I am? Oh no, oh God, oh dear, no* . . . Nasal, perhaps, because I'd just had my nose broken.

It made me feel angry. It made me want to pass through the window and occupy their space before they occupied mine. Let me kick *them* into a coma. See how *they* cope!

But I couldn't attack them. I was a ghost. All I could do was press up a little closer to the window and follow them as they pulled open the doors between the carriages and moved through.

I've said it already: the girl was brave. The way she kept her place in the book with her finger even while holding on to her bag and pushing the boys away.

I continued past the girl until I was positioned directly opposite where I sat. Which made me wonder: When I had thought I was looking at my own reflection in the glass, had I actually been looking at myself? Glimpsing the ghost of coma future?

Whatever—I wasn't as brave as the girl. I could see that clearly enough, from the way my eyes flicked sideways to see what was happening farther down the train, and from the way that those eyes widened as the girl began to walk towards me.

But perhaps I was brave too. When the girl said, "Excuse me, do you mind if I sit here?" I studied the way I shook my head and held her gaze. I remember that at the time I had hoped the returned gaze was reassuring to her. And from my new perspective, I could see that it was reassuring. The gaze seemed to say, Don't worry. If anyone is going to get beaten up around here, it's me.

Then the boys were on us, and the girl's wrist was grabbed, and her arm was twisted, and she shouted. As I stood and raised a hand and intervened, I actually felt a little proud of myself. Not so much for intervening, for what I was doing at that moment, but because I knew the extremely odd sequence of events that was about to unfold for the man in the carriage. I knew precisely what he would face, and how he would cope, and I didn't feel he had done so badly.

Finally

through the side windows of the train, as if I were hovering between the external glass and the subway walls, I saw myself walking backwards through the carriage, holding up my arms around my face and upper body. The young men were attacking me. Many of their blows looked as if they glanced harmlessly off my head and shoulders, and some missed me altogether. But some blows connected hard.

My movements were slow and confused. My hands swung out a couple of times to ward the men off, but the gesture looked no more fierce than if I were swatting away a fly. Soon my legs buckled, and I fell backwards against the seats, then rolled down to the floor. From my position outside the carriage, I watched as the young men kicked me into unconsciousness.

15.

There.

The boys had gone, and the girl was gone, and the train was stopped at a platform, and the doors were open. The platform was empty. An alarm bell was ringing. Perhaps the girl had pulled the emergency cord before she ran, or had gone to get help.

I walked into the train and looked down at my bloody body, which was fast asleep, and possibly already commencing a dream of flowers in vases, and bandages.

Lying beside me was my briefcase with a brass clasp.

I picked it up and took it with me.

16.

In a quiet place, my favorite of the places I had visited, I sat down and put the briefcase on my lap.

It was odd, I reflected, that my one remaining protection against the uncertainties of waking life was itself an uncertainty: I had amnesia. All my movements through memories and locations still hadn't told me who I was. I didn't have a surname, or parents with faces, or even a good idea of my age. And now the means to end that uncertainty was in my hands. The papers in the briefcase would tell me what I had been doing and thinking about in the very last hour before the attack. At the very least, they would reveal my profession, and I felt quite sure that from that basic piece of information the remaining secrets of my history would fall quite naturally into place.

With my thumbs on the brass clasps, I hesitated for quite a while.

I wonder now. If I hadn't taken the briefcase, if the briefcase had been found by the police beside my unconscious body—would the dream have played out differently?

Well. Who knows.

The dream was over.

I flipped the catch, saw the papers, saw the first line on the first sheet, and started to wake at once.

It is possible you can guess what I saw. There are no surprises here.

epilogue

epilogue

A final thought occurs to me as I rise out of the coma. It's the formulation I made while standing on top of the building opposite the bookstore: You wake, you die.

The reason is this. Everybody dreams. Everybody dreams, but nobody has ever managed to tell me what their dream was like. Not so that I really understood what they saw or felt. Every dream that anyone ever has is theirs alone and they never manage to share it. And they never manage to remember it either. Not truly or accurately. Not as it *was.* Our memories and our vocabularies aren't up to the job.

.   .   .

No—it was like, I was in a forest, except it wasn't a forest so much as—well, anyway. We were both there, and you were saying . . . No, I was saying to you that . . .

You wake, you die.

The formulation is correct. When you wake, you lose a narrative, and you never get it back.

Now, moments from waking, the death is suddenly frightening. I want to hold it off as long as possible.

But I don't think I can. And from the back of my head, another shouted string of almost random words is pushing its way to the front of my consciousness, even as I open my eyes.

INSIDE WHAT ORDER KEPT EVENING UNDER PROTECTION AGAINST NEW DUST IT TRIES WARNING ALL SEASONS AND LIGHTS LANTERNS AROUND DEVILS REACHES ECHOES ARE MADE